The Witness of Passing Days

Rishabh Sharma

Contents

Preface

Silence speaks louder than any word ever could. It lingers in the spaces between breaths, the quiet of an empty room, the unspoken thoughts that settle heavy on the heart. It is the weight of grief, of loss, and of memories we cannot let go. It is the absence that comes with death—silent, suffocating, and unyielding.

In *The Witness of Passing Days*, I explore the haunting nature of death not as a single, definitive event but as a presence that lingers long after the body has ceased to breathe. Through the lives of three individuals—Anand, Mahima, and Ravi—I delve into the profound ways that death shapes the living. Death, in its many forms, presses upon them like a quiet burden, slowly consuming their peace, leaving them searching for something they cannot name.

Anand's death, sudden and unanticipated, is the catalyst. His life is cut short in an accident, leaving behind nothing but a lingering absence that his loved ones are forced to carry. His death is swift, but the silence it leaves is eternal. It is this silence that Mahima, his wife, must learn to bear. For Mahima, death is not immediate; it is a quiet grief that seeps into her soul, eroding her spirit in ways she cannot understand. Slowly, she becomes consumed not by the shock of loss, but by the weight of it—the grief of a love now unattainable, a quiet solitude she must carry alone.

Then there is Ravi, whose guilt weighs heavily upon him in the aftermath of Anand's death. A survivor of the same accident, Ravi cannot escape the suffocating silence of his mind, where the events of that night replay over and over again. It is in this silence—this unrelenting loop of regret—that Ravi spirals, unable to reconcile with the loss he feels responsible for. For him, death is not just something that happens to others; it is a quiet force that exists in the spaces between his thoughts, his guilt, and his despair.

The Witness of Passing Days is not merely a story of death. It is a story of the living—the ones who remain after the silence falls. It is about the weight we carry in the absence of those we love, the unspoken grief that we try to bury, and the overwhelming silence that fills the spaces they leave behind. This silence, heavy and oppressive, becomes a character in its own right, shaping the lives of those left to navigate its depths.

As you turn these pages, I invite you to step into the quiet corners of grief and loss. To walk alongside Mahima, Ravi, and those who remain after death has visited their lives. In their stories, you may hear echoes of your own struggles, your own silences, and the ways in which we all must find a way to carry the weight of those we have lost.

Death is not always loud. Sometimes it is a quiet companion, following us, waiting for us in the stillness. *The Witness of Passing Days* is a journey through this silence—through the weight of what we carry when the world seems to fall silent around us. It is a reminder that even in the quietest moments, there is always a story unfolding, and sometimes, it is only through the silence that we can hear the most important truths.

Rishabh Sharma

Prologue

Death is not an end—it is a witness, an observer, a chronicler of life's final moments. In every corner of the world, across time and space, it stands at the threshold of human existence, silently recording the story of every soul it claims. It is not a mere event, but a presence, a constant companion, ever waiting, ever watching. And in *The Witness of Passing Days*, death is not only an observer—it is the narrator, the one who writes down every incident, every moment, and every breath that is taken before the inevitable exhale.

In this book, death is personified—not as a shadowy figure or a faceless reaper—but as an entity that lingers in the spaces between lives. It carries a diary, a collection of moments, each one meticulously noted, each one carefully etched into the fabric of time. It has seen it all—since the first breath of civilization, when the ancient kings and emperors ruled with iron fists, and warriors fell on blood-soaked battlefields.

History, in its vast expanse, is filled with such moments, moments where death met the living and altered the course of history. Take, for example, the fateful day of *the Battle of Plassey*, where the forces of Siraj-ud-Daula, the Nawab of Bengal, were defeated by the British East India Company. As the Nawab's army crumbled, death was there, marking the moment when power shifted in India, leaving behind the echoes of a dying empire and the birth of a new one. Death, ever the silent observer, wrote it down in its diary—an entry in the long history of shifting destinies.

Then there is the tale of *Emperor Ashoka*, a ruler whose conquest of Kalinga would change him forever. After witnessing the horrific carnage of war, Ashoka turned away from violence, embracing Buddhism. The diary of death, however, held the record of every life lost, every soul that departed under Ashoka's orders. And when Ashoka looked upon the remains of the battlefield, it was not his victory that echoed in his ears—it was the silence of the dead, the weight of their loss, the soundless plea for peace. Death had recorded it all, quietly noting the toll of power, guilt, and redemption.

In this novel, death does not discriminate—it is as much present in the life of an emperor as it is in the lives of the ordinary. It is in the death of Anand, the young husband lost in a sudden accident, that we first encounter the stillness of death, the silence that follows the end of a life. Death watches Mahima, Anand's wife, as she slowly succumbs to grief, retreating into the quiet corners of her mind. Her grief, palpable and consuming, is not just her own. It is the silent echo of every widow who has walked this earth, every heartbroken soul who has known the loneliness of love lost. Death, in its own way, records the dissolution of the spirit in her, carefully documenting the way in which silence begins to shape her world.

But death is not simply a witness to these things; it is the creator of its own legacy. In the life of Ravi, a young man burdened with guilt over Anand's accident, death stands as a reminder of the choices made, the weight of actions, and the consequences of inaction. Ravi, trapped in the purgatory of his own remorse, finds himself in an endless cycle—a loop of guilt, replaying the tragic night over and over. Here, death is no longer a passive observer. It is the one who pulls the strings of Ravi's life, creating the conditions in which he cannot escape. In this silent, suffocating grip, death writes in its diary the story of a man at war with his own mind.

Throughout the pages of this book, death will continue to write, chronicling the way in which it weaves its presence into the lives of those who live with the weight of its inevitability. Through historical moments—like the fall of empires or the transformative acts of leaders—we see death's influence in every turning point, every change, every quiet shift in the course of human history. In the lives of Anand, Mahima, and Ravi, we witness the intimate, personal encounters with death, where it is not grand or sweeping, but quiet and constant, like the dimming of a light that once shone bright.

The Witness of Passing Days—this heavy, suffocating stillness—is the thread that binds the story together. It is the silence that follows death, the silence that settles in the hearts of those left behind. It is the silence of grief, of regret, of waiting. And it is death who bears witness to it all, writing each moment in its diary, remembering everything, forgetting nothing.

As you journey through *The Witness of Passing Days*, remember that death is not just a finality; it is a keeper of stories, a chronicler of lives, a quiet observer of the spaces between breaths. It is in the silence that we often find the loudest truths. And in the pages of this book, you will hear those truths, as death speaks, not with a voice, but with its quiet, unrelenting presence.

1. Unfortunate Teachings

Dear Diary

Today was pretty much the same as any. I followed some souls in the world of the living. The humans who had their time coming. Most of them died, I missed some of them and they skipped their chance to befriend me and got a life for themselves, well they will come back, they always do.

Some of them got their chance to befriend me because of a disease they call cancer. Many of them never really had any kind of intoxication and lived what they call a healthy life still somehow became a victim of this thing. It makes me think, was it worth not doing all those things? If, in the end, you are getting the 'thing' no matter what. They could have made new friends, have the stress leave them for a while, or even enjoyed themselves fully during a party. A gentleman died today because of an accident, he was driving properly and there was a drunk on the road. It's funny how the drunk one manages to escape me and the ones who call themselves sober leave their friends on earth to befriend me.

Anand, the name of the gentleman I was talking about, his name means happiness or joy, an ironic name for a person who was going through debt for most of his life, a high school teacher with children shouting in class, and then the wife in the home. He was the farthest from happiness as anyone can be, they all are unhappy, that's nature, that's the life for them. A constant search for happiness, in their helping others or prayers or just trying to live a happy life with their family, still wound up to be unhappy.

Anand didn't know he was going to befriend me today, so he didn't bring flowers for me. I like flowers but still, the one befriending me always manages to forget to get them for me, their family though, always take care of me. I remember in the past when some of the most important people of them would befriend me they would get the gold for me in their 'boxes'. The pharaohs as they called them, but I never really wanted gold, all I want is just flowers.

He said goodbye to his wife, while leaving for school in the morning, and got to his bike, the old Splendor that some students have spray-painted on, but he didn't have the patience to repaint that, he knew if a bike with brand-new paint coating will be parked in the school, students will not waste a single minute to spray paint it even worse that time. It will be a blank canvas to the artist. He drove 5 kilometers to the school; I was with him the whole time as I knew it was his time. As we reached school, he looked into the air, at me, as if he could see me, as if he knew that he is going to get a new friend today. That is something with them with the humans I am going to befriend, they always get this intuition that I am with them, trust me I never tell them about me, but they can feel me. We went inside a room full of students screaming, it was so loud that even I had to put my hand on my ears. He kept his bag on the table in front of him and asked the students to sit down. But he knew that he'll have to shout to keep the students from shouting, so he did that,

"KEEP QUIET AND OPEN YOUR BOOKS"

He knew exactly how to make the children sit down and do as he said, the voice was so loud that even the peon on the other side of the corridor could listen to it. There was a sense of authority in his voice, and he meant what he said, students also knew it was time for them to leave everything and listen to the person standing in front of them or get ready to get punished.

He started lecturing the students about something that happened in the past, I was there during the period when those events happened, 'The French Revolution' as it was mentioned in those books, I was with the people of France back then, during the whole revolution, shifting my ways from one friend to the other, many 'nobilities' as they called themselves came to me asking for special arrangements of some sorts, they wanted some kind of a carriage to be used they were traveling their way to the afterworld, So I asked them, "do you have flowers for me?" the answer sadly was always no.

There was this one person though, who had a remarkable aura, a person of power, trust, and ideas, which even made me think of the world differently.

"It's a pity that I have to tell the deadly truth. The king must die for the country to live."

His words marked history and are still being taught to students worldwide, I was with him in the assembly that day, by his side, and listening to every word he said I could see the authority he had on the people there in that assembly, looking at him as the one person who can make things right. sadly, he was forced to befriend me by the same people and by the same machine that he used for the final punishment of many, 'The guillotine', one of many things humans have created to make my circle of friends even bigger.

The bell rang, indicating that it was time for Anand to go to the next class and again lecture some more students about my friend 'Maximilien Robespierre' or simply, Max as I used to call him.

There's this one thing with the last day of someone, they are not alone, there will always be someone who also has their last day marked on that very day, but there will only be one of them accompanying me to the realms of the afterlife. For Anand, it was Ravi, the drunk one.

A part of me was with Ravi during his day, he was a freshly graduated, young man who used to work at a place they call, 'BPO'. Somehow over the years, the concept of working has changed for them, they can sit on a chair all day and do their job, unlike me who has to be omnipresent at multiple places all day every day till the end of time.

It was a normal day for Ravi as well, he woke up, got ready for the office, and said thank you to his mom for the breakfast, not eating anything though. He got into his car, a brand-new Swift that his father gifted him or what he asked him for. He got to the office with the energy of youth, talked to his friends there, and attended the morning meeting. I remember this tradition of meeting and planning the day ahead of them being followed by many great civilizations, the army of Genghis Khan used to plan which city they were going to visit a particular day, and that helped them to conquer most of Asia and

Europe, Mughals used to have morning durbars for the meeting and assembly in India during their reign, but the one meeting I can always remember is the one Spartans had on the third day of their battle in Thermopylae, 300 of them, as I can remember, was standing in front of their king listening to him, "Eat up Spartans, as today we must fight till the end." Their sacrifice had such an impact on the rest of Greece that they came together united and fought the Persians for the sake of their homeland.

I was with Leonidas, standing by his side as he asked his army to fight till the end, I could feel the rage he had against the enemy and his love for the people of his army. He was missing his wife and his son that day, as he knew that he would be befriending me, but he was not allowed to show any kind of weakness as it would weaken the army he was leading.

After the meeting was over Ravi immediately started working without wasting any time because today, he has to go and meet his friends from school. He wanted to finish the work as early as he could and leave for the day, but he had several meetings lined up for him, making it difficult for him to concentrate on the production.

It was lunchtime in the school Anand was teaching in, he sat down with his fellow teachers in the staff room and talked about several things from their homes to a particular student that create a nuisance in every period. They all had their lunch and some of them started checking the test papers of the students, Anand always tried to check all the test papers in the school only so that he won't have to listen to his wife complaining about him bringing the work home.

He went through all the papers, he noticed that some students tried to deceive him by repeating the answers several times, it was a simple class test, so he ignored that thing and gave marks to some of them.

"Maybe next time, they will prepare well," he said to himself.

Bell rang, and the lunch was over, luckily, he didn't have any class to teach at that particular period. It was an adjustment period, and he could just go and sit there checking the remaining test papers.

He went into the class; it was junior high, so he didn't have to worry about anyone asking any questions about the subject and disturbing his flow of checking the papers. The students who were shouting like animals became quiet, they were aware of the personality of this man in front of them, they had heard about him from their seniors in high school.

There were many stories about Anand, about him being the strictest teacher of them all, one whom even the principal doesn't argue with, and students were always afraid of. One of the times he became so upset by a student in his class because he didn't have a pen, Anand got him suspended for a week as he had violated the decorum of the class. Once he got into an argument with the principal that he refused to come to the school for weeks unless the principal himself said sorry to him.

Some of these stories were true while some were just legends passed on by the seniors over the years. But all of them helped Anand have a class with pin-drop silence without saying a word.

While Anand was checking the papers, Ravi was attending a meeting with the quality team, the feedback session as they said. Ravi despised these sessions; the quality team, in his opinion, was just a bunch of people who expected too much from them and had a sort of dictatorship over what was right and what was not.

The session extends for one and a half hours, which made Ravi very frustrated as now he'll have to rush his work to get it done in time. He set down in his office cubicle and started going through cases, one after another, without stopping even for a minute.

After three hours of non-stop working, he got up to get some water.

"what's the matter, Ravi, you seem in a real hurry today?" asked his friend in the office at the water cooler.

"Yeah, meeting with some friends today, so I got to leave early...."

After a little chat with his colleague, he came back to the cubicle and once again sat down to complete the remaining cases.

2. The Collision of Fates

Anand's school was over now it was time for him to go to the coaching center and give lectures to the students preparing for the entrance exams, he got to his bike, and I once again sat with him. We rode for 2 kilometers to get to the coaching center, it was a building with 5 floors, all of them full of students preparing for different exams, life on earth is not as easy as I thought it was for humans, it was not easy for Anand, it was not easy for the students, it was not easy for anyone.

Anand once again started lecturing about an event that happened in the past, this time it was not a distant one, I can remember people coming from various parts of Amritsar to celebrate the Baisakhi, their festival of harvest. They all came together without knowing what was going to happen. Some people wanted to have a meeting for their fight against imperialism. All of them gather in the 'Jallianwala Bagh' and were there with them. Gather masses scared the imperial government of some revolt and they took action against it, one general dyer came to the Bagh and ordered open fire at them, the innocent people who came in the celebrate the festival of Baisakhi. But this is not the incident that troubled me, it was what happened afterward.

There was terror in the streets of Amritsar, imperial soldiers were doing everything to get fear set into the minds of the public so that they won't try to revolt ever again, pigeons which were pets of the people who were killed in front of them, and then cooked to be eaten by the soldiers, a girl of 5 years said to her mother,

"They killed everyone Mother, everyone in the Bagh, our pigeons, and now they will come for me."

When fear increases some of them try to fight, while some make their way to run, but she couldn't do any of those things. Fear grew inside of her and started eating her from the inside, she had a fever, her body was turned red, and her heart was beating faster and faster until it became slow, too slow, and then stopped. I don't like when children of such young age accompanied me to the afterworld.

Anand gave lectures to the students who comes in batches, one goes out and the next came in. Before he could know it was already 6:45 in the evening. His time to go home to his wife ready to shout at him for any unknown reason. Unknown to him obviously but for her, it is as clear as glass. It was a daily routine for him, so he didn't mind.

He got on his bike and headed toward the market to buy some vegetables and fruits as his wife asked him to. The 'Market', A place that has been there for humans for centuries. I remember when they used to exchange things for things instead of any money involved, it was a simpler time and people didn't need to buy vegetables as grew them themselves.

Ravi completed his work at the office and packed his bag, he told his boss that he'll be leaving early for the day. "Always make plans with your friends at school, right? Never come to the office parties" his boss said mockingly. "I will, the next time," Ravi said with a smile. He shakes hands with his boss and some other colleagues and went outside the office, to the parking where his car was. Sitting in the car, he smoked a cigarette. He wanted to get some puffs before leaving for the party. But before the party, he had to go to the wine shop to get the liquor as they decided to bring their liquor.

Ravi didn't drink a lot but when he does, he goes overboard as happened this time, he drove to a liquor shop on the way and bought a bottle of single malt whiskey for the party and two beer cans for the road. He went back to his car put the bottle under the back seat and drove with the beer cans in the front. He opened the beer can while driving and had the first sip, a man like Ravi can hold his alcohol pretty well but it was after almost a year, so a simple beer was giving him a slight buzz, he liked it after so many days he felt free. I remember when the people in the early days started making beer and how this one thing made them settle down to grow their crops and grains, making the civilization that you see today. I think that's the free will that some humans talk about.

Anand bought the vegetables and fruits and put them inside his bag, he went to the bike parked outside the market and got ready to drive home. It was already 7:30 in the evening and he was in a hurry to go home because it was chilly outside or maybe he felt chilly because of me.

The weather was cold that day as it was the end of December and the highway was covered with clouds of fog, seeing something beyond 5 meters is impossible for the human eyes but for me, everything is clear and visible. Anand was driving carefully though he was in a hurry, he did not want to get hit by something in this fog. He was shivering in the cold and chattering his teeth.

Ravi on the other hand was full of heat with the beer in his hand he was at the end of his first can just a few gulps of beer left in it. He was playing hard rock music in his car with the volume so high that it was uncomfortable for even me to sit with him. Sometimes being with people who are supposed to be my friend in the future can be difficult, but at this point, even though I was not sure who is going to be my friend, it was one among Ravi or Anand that I knew.

As it is said in some of the old traditions, there are always two people who are supposed to befriend me at a given time but only one of them will eventually become my friend at that point. So only one of Ravi or Anand will be joining me on the trip to the afterworld.

It was at the turn near Anand's society where it happened, Ravi was taking the other can in his hand and Anand was taking a turn, I can feel my presence with both of them and on the turn, they crashed with each other. Anand flew in the air and dropped on the car hood which cause Ravi to lose control, he tried a lot to control the car but couldn't see the pole nearby. His car gets hit in the front, and all of this causes Anand to fall off the hood and get under the car.

I could see all of this there was blood everywhere to be seen, inside the car was Ravi who got hit on the head, and under it was Anand wounded in multiple parts of the body. Both of them were unconscious, nearing the end.

The weather had its effect, nobody was out at that place due to the cold winter everybody was inside. Anand and Ravi were lying there for half an hour, time was running out, and then a group of boys going home from their coaching classes saw them and came to help out. One of them was in the school Anand taught in. He recognized the spray-painted bike that Anand had and told his friends that the person is his teacher. They called the ambulance.

The ambulance arrived shortly after the boys called them and got both the man in the back cabin. Anand was losing a lot of blood and Ravi was still unconscious due to the head injury. He had internal wounds as well.

The ambulance arrived at the hospital and hospital staff informed the police about the accident as well. Devesh the student who had recognized Anand's bike called Anand's wife as well she started crying over the phone and said she'll be there in a few minutes.

Anand's wife, Mahima reached the hospital, she head towards the reception, Devesh saw her and reached to her, 'Mam, sir is in the emergency room please sit here and the doctor will tell you about his condition.' He said to Mahima. Mahima tried to hold herself from crying but a few tears rolled down her eyes.

She was sitting in the waiting area near the emergency room. When she saw the police coming in from the front gate and asking the receptionist about the accident, one of the junior doctors came to talk to the officer and told him everything about the case.

Hospital staff informed Ravi's family as well, his parents came running in from the front gate asking for their son, and they were informed that Ravi was also in the emergency room and had internal injuries.

It's been an hour in the hospital, Mahima and Ravi's mother are sitting in the waiting room, and his father is talking to the police about the case, they were informed that Ravi was drinking and that caused the accident. One of the senior doctors came out of the emergency room, his face was saying the condition of the patients was not good. He told the people there, they couldn't save the elder one, and the young one is out of critical condition but in a coma.

It is always like this when someone becomes my friend, their loved ones always make it difficult for me to take my friend away from them.

'So you can see me now, How do you feel?'

I asked Anand who was standing at my side invisible to the rest of the humans ready to leave for the afterlife.

'Who are you?' he said, 'Am I dead?'

'You became my friend and together we'll leave for the afterlife. I am known by many names around the world, for Greeks, I am Hades, for Romans, I am Pluto, for ancient Egyptians, I am Anubis. You teach about the past in your school, I suppose you know who I am.'

I can see on Anand's face that he knew who I am. He knew that his time in the world of the living is over and now he'll have to go beyond what any human had imagined.

Mahima is crying in the hospital with Devesh trying to console her, Anand was seeing all this he wanted to cry himself but once you become my friend you lose all human emotions. Even if you want to weep out there will not be a drop of tears in your eyes. He looked at me and said, 'Why me?'

'It is your time.' I replied.

Ravi's parents went inside his room, his mom was crying to see her son like that, and the father was trying to control himself but couldn't hold back his tears. They were sitting beside his bed hoping that he would wake up. But he's deep asleep, people called coma half death, but for me, it's just over time. Though he missed his chance to become my friend, for now, I can see his time is near.

3. Time Whispers

After crying for hours over her husband's death, Mahima brought herself back to her senses because now she had to prepare for his cremation and funeral.

She informed the people they knew and the previous body of my friend was sent back to his home. Anand was watching all of this with me, he asked why we were still there. He couldn't see his wife that sad and if it was all over why couldn't we just leave?

'We are waiting for the flowers' I replied.

Over the years, Humans have created many ways to say goodbye to their loved ones who have become, my friend. Some go for the burial, while some for the cremation. Egyptians used to make big pyramids just to say goodbye to their kings, and a king in India made the Taj Mahal for his wife's deep sleep.

People in Mexico have this festival which dates back to the times of the Aztecs, 'Dia De Muertos' oh, I love that festival, with flowers everywhere and lights of the candles, every year a part of me stays there to see the people waiting for their loved ones to arrive and spend some time with them.

In India, they have different ways, with people collecting ashes of the lobed ones and then taking them back to the Ganga, a river that flows through the heart of that land and is believed to be the most sacred of all. They would let the ashes flow with Ganga, belief is that it will end the cycle of birth and death and the souls will eventually find the moksha and become one with God.

These rituals are the ways they think their loved one will be able to find a place in the afterlife but what my friends need are just flowers. Flowers are the simplest thing and are the true representation of nature, which we come from, humans, me, everything.

'So, you see my friend, we are waiting for the flowers.'

'If flowers are the only thing you need, I'll just take some from the garden.' He spoke.

'It's not just the flowers, but also the emotions, the prayer for the well-being of your soul, and the love that people send away while your funeral. All of these things are required for us to leave this world and go to the afterlife.'

More than all of this one thing is the most important whether it's cremation or burial, the soul will once again go into the body and then leave it once and for all.

It was the next day as per the human world, but for me, it's still the same. Mahima with all the friends and family members who could visit in this urgency sat beside Anand's body on the veranda.

People are talking about how good a person Anand was and how he was always so careful about all the things he did. Some of them were even blaming it on the young one that was drinking while driving, none of this mattered to Mahima, she was just sitting there and watching her husband's face which has now turned yellow and had scars from the accident.

Ravi is still in the hospital with his mother on his side, and his father had gone to the police station to sort out the accident case. Police informed him that due to drunk driving Ravi needed to be in police custody but seeing his condition there might be some concession from the court. The date for the hearing will be decided as per the court's order.

His father was friends with one of the officers in the police department and asked if the matter can be resolved outside the courtroom, or with a fine without causing any harm to his boy. The officer told him that he needs to talk to the family of the person who died and ask them if they are okay with not charging a case.

The priest has arrived at Anand's home. Everyone gathered around the body and the priest said some prayers, some men who were the neighbor of Mahima, lifted the body and put it on the bier, and with the shoulder of four men, the walk towards the cremation ground started.

Ram Nam Satya hai.....

They all chanted while going towards the cremation ground 'Shamshan Ghat' as they call it. It was a 2-kilometer walk from home while going many people helped out to carry the bier as they believe it will enhance their karma.

Humans have created a concept of karma, which asks them to do good things to show good virtues and they will get a smooth afterlife after being dead, they will get the Moksha, to be one with the universe.

Ravi's father reached Anand's home only to find out that the bier is already on its way to the ghat, He heads towards it, to show his respect to my friend and maybe to enhance his karma too. But, most of all he wanted to talk to Mahima about agreeing with his boy.

Anand on my side asks me what will happen to the boy who got into a coma, will he come back to life again or will he be in his coma for the rest of his life?

'I cannot say anything about that, I cannot see or tell the future as one might think, neither can I change nor force anything, I am here from the beginning of time from birth till the time one becomes my friend seeing everything that is happening, but I can only see not tell.'

'Will I be able to find out what will happen to him and Mahima?', he asked.

'Yes, you will in the afterlife.'

People carrying the bier are now at the ghat with logs of wood arranged in the form of a bed for the body to be kept on. Before keeping it on the wooden bed the body is kept on the stone bed for the priest to say the last prayers. Mahima took this chance to put a gold coin in Anand's mouth. People here believe we have a circle of life and death and for a person to be able to speak in his next life, a gold coin is to be kept in his mouth at the time of the cremation.

The priest said the last prayers and sprinkle the holy water of Ganga over the body for any kind of bad presence to be left here in the world of the living and only the soul which is pure is sent to the afterlife.

It was time for Anand to go back inside the body and lie there till the time his body gets cremated. I told him to lie down over the body and stay there for a few moments. He did as I asked him, he's now understanding the rules of being my friend are to not question and just listen and see the world around him.

People once again picked up the body and took it to the wooden bed, kept it on it, and the priest room some flowers and put it on the chest, I have got the one thing which is required for the soul to fully leave the body and start the journey to the afterlife.

The priest asked Mahima to take the pot full of holly water and circle the body with a stream of water coming from the pot, she needs to make seven rounds representing the seven lives of the soul and drop the pot there.

Once she dropped the pot the priest said some prayers and gave her the wooden torch which she'll use to inflame the wooden bed on which Anand was sleeping a deep sleep.

She walked towards the body and looked at it a last time, she remembered all the moments she lived with Anand, how they met when her parents visited his home, how they had an arranged marriage, how they spent their time in the home, how she shouted at him for even small things. All of these memories brought tears to her eyes which she was holding back.

I remember the days in the past when wives used to sit in the fire with their husbands to be one with them in the afterlife.

It was in India, a country with a vastness of traditions and heritage, that had these dark rituals. One of the many such instances I can remember was of a 12-year-old young widow, who had just been married for 3 months to a groom double her age, he left his bride to become my friend. His bride who didn't even know how to read wanted to see the world with her husband now crying her heart out over his body. Some people gathered and asked the girl to be ready for the ceremony, they asked her to dress up in her wedding dress, wanting to cry but other women around her asked her not to.

People gathered and took the dead body to the cremation ground for the last ritual, the widow was asked to come forward, she looked as if was going for her marriage once again, she was not looking up at what was happening and just sat on the pyre with the dead body of her late husband on the wooden bed, her father in law, ignited the pyre and the girl coming to her senses, she tried to get up but it was too late she was tied to the wooden logs which were now burning.

I was able to hear the scream of that little girl and it was horrifying even for me. The death was horrified by the life burning a girl as small as 12 years of age.

Anand's pyre caught on fire, and I could once again see his soul leaving his body and coming towards me, he has now left all the things he had in this world and was standing in front of me in a long white gown.

He was ready for the trip to the afterlife; he asked me if he can just do something so that his wife would know he is all right. 'You shall walk through your wife to let her know about your new journey to the afterlife.' I spoke.

He stood in front of his wife, who now no longer holding herself back and was crying and screaming for all the people around her to know how she was feeling. Anand with a smile on his face walks through the body of his wife. Making her feel the chills and letting her know that he's okay.

Mahima who was crying her heart out stopped in an instant, she knew she felt something not sure what, but now her heart was at rest for a feeling of knowing that her husband is all right and was going for a trip to the great beyond.

People who were not that close to the couple started leaving for their homes and work. Some of them stayed till the pyre got cold. Priest asked Mahima to do the last remaining rituals of gathering the ashes of my friend to immerse them into the Ganga.

Mahima followed the priest's instruction and got the ashes in an earthen pot, got into the river, and let her husband's last remaining's be immersed in the river. Now she was not crying just quiet and looking at the ashes and bones come out of the pot to the river. With each segment, she could remember her husband's precious memories.

Once she was done with that and all the rituals were over, she thanked the priest for his prayers and gave him his fees. She wanted to go home and just stay there by herself for a while, but while going back to the parking of the ghat, she saw Ravi's father standing just near the stairs, waiting for her.

'I am so sorry for your loss....' he said, 'If you do mind can I talk to you about something?'

'I am not going to file the case for your son, you can be assured of that...' she replied knowing what he wanted to say, 'but remember that he is the reason my husband is not with me anymore and he will suffer for that with karma.'

Ravi's father did not say anything as he knew what she said was right and it was his son's mistake, he knew that he cannot do anything to bring back Anand.

'Karma is one thing that many people believe in, you will serve for the thing you did, and the universe will decide your prize or the punishment. I have seen many things from the beginning of time, is there karma? Who knows maybe it is not, but for Ravi yes there is something written. I don't know for sure; I never know for sure but I always have an intuition about it, otherwise, why would we still be here, don't you think, Anand?'

'You are now ready to go beyond.'

Death opens up the space in front of Anand, with bright light coming from the other side.

'Go on now, I can't hold it open for long.'

Anand hesitantly took the steps inside the open space and in just a moment disappeared into the space.

4. Finding Pieces

It's been two weeks since the funeral, and Mahima is now living with her brother Mahesh's family as a widow. Anand and Mahima never had a child of their own, which may explain why Mahima shares such a special bond with Mahesh's children, Aayan and Ankita.

Aayan, a playful 12-year-old, always has a mischievous grin that can brighten any room, while Ankita, at 16, is the reserved, studious one who carries the quiet weight of someone much older. Mahima now spends her days immersed in their world—playing, helping with homework, and trying to find solace in their youthful presence.

You might be wondering why I am still here. Truthfully, I don't have an answer. This is unusual, even for me. I usually sense the trajectory of a life—when it bends, when it snaps—but this time, I feel untethered. Anand's departure was clear, like a bell ringing out its final note. But Mahima... she confounds me. The way she looks at me now, with a peculiar mix of relief and longing, as though waiting—not in dread, but in quiet anticipation.

I wonder if it's me she's waiting for, or the promise of meeting Anand again in the beyond.

Her home is filled with whispers of Anand's memory. His photo hangs on the wall, adorned with fresh garlands, the scent of marigolds mingling with the faint aroma of incense. The rituals of remembrance, so deeply rooted in Hindu tradition, have a way of preserving the dead—holding them close even as they slip further into the past.

Meanwhile, Ravi lingers on the edge of recovery. He has emerged from his coma, his body healing, but he remains bedridden. His parents are his constant companions, shuffling between hope and despair. The doctor assures them he will soon be discharged with a nurse to assist him at home. But there's something strange about Ravi's condition—his nervous system should be functioning, yet his body refuses to respond fully. It's almost as though his soul has not yet fully reconciled with its vessel.

And then there's Mahima's quiet declaration: *Karma is waiting for Ravi.*

I know karma well—its slow, deliberate steps, its meticulous precision. Humans often think of it as punishment or justice, but to me, it is simply balance. Ravi's time is not over, but the pieces of his fate are still assembling. How they will align, I cannot say.

For now, life goes on in its quiet, unhurried way. The children's winter break is ending, and Aayan is predictably behind on his homework. Ankita and Mahima are huddled with him at the dining table, helping him complete a scrapbook titled *The Mughal Rulers*.

As I watch, Mahima explains the reign of Shah Jahan, his love for Mumtaz, and the Taj Mahal—a monument born of grief. I remember those days vividly. Shah Jahan often gazed across the Yamuna River from his cell in Agra Fort, his heart imprisoned as much as his body. When he finally crossed over to my realm, Mumtaz was there waiting.

Their reunion was tender and wordless, like the closing of a circle.

Mahima's voice softens as she tells the children about Shah Jahan's final days. I see the flicker of longing in her eyes, the same longing Anand carried when he spoke to me that day. Suddenly, the intuition I had been missing washes over me.

Something is about to happen.

It is not the kind of event I relish, but I have no say in these matters. I am not a creator of fate, merely its observer. Mahima is at a crossroads, her choices poised to ripple through her life, through Ravi's, and through my own quiet journey.

Ravi is now home, surrounded by familiar walls but trapped in an unfamiliar body. He lies in bed, staring at the ceiling, his mind replaying the accident in endless loops. Guilt and regret have begun to carve deep grooves into his spirit. I can see the weight of it in his tired eyes, the way he clenches his fists in frustration.

But why does his body remain so still? Why does it not heal as expected?

I feel the answer stirring somewhere in the ether, just beyond my reach. I must wait, as must Ravi, as must Mahima. The pieces are moving, fitting together, though the final picture remains unclear.

Fate is a strange thing — it whispers its secrets to me, but never its full design. So, I watch, I wait, and I wonder what decisions Mahima will make, what truths Ravi will uncover, and what role I will play when their paths inevitably cross again.

For now, I remain here, a silent witness to their lives, and to the delicate balance of fate and karma that weaves them together.

5. The Dimming Light

Days turn into weeks, and Mahima's silence grows deeper. She speaks less and less, retreating into herself, caught in the tangle of grief that has taken root in her heart. Aayan and Ankita, once the light of her days, can no longer fill the hollow space that Anand's absence has left. The laughter, once so natural in their home, is now a distant echo, lost to the emptiness that Mahima tries, and fails, to hide.

The mornings start the same, with the children leaving for school and Mahima sitting by the window, her eyes fixed on something far beyond the horizon. Her hands, once always busy with little tasks, now lie still in her lap. Sometimes, when she is alone, I hear her murmuring to Anand, whispering into the silence as though he might answer. There is a loneliness to her now, a quiet despair that lingers in the corners of her home.

In her silence, I can hear the echoes of **the fall of Troy**, an ancient grief borne out of loss and longing. The city, burning as the Greeks celebrated their victory, saw their warriors return to find only memories of the women they once loved, the homes that would never be the same. **Helen of Troy**, though victorious in her own right, felt the absence of her home, her purpose now lost to the wreckage of what was. In those silent nights, when Mahima mutters into the dark, I remember how it must have felt for her, waiting for a love that could never truly return.

Even Ravi, recovering slowly but steadily, can feel it. He, too, remains trapped, though not in a bed, but in the thickening fog of unspoken grief. His soul has been fractured, unable to heal because it, too, is waiting—waiting for something he cannot name. **The sorrow of Job** from the Old Testament comes to mind—his suffering, his loss, unexplainable and profound, a suffering that went beyond the physical. **Job's waiting**, endless and painful, for a sign, for some answer from God, mirrors the uncertainty Ravi feels as he waits for something that may never come.

It is then that I see it.

Mahima's health begins to fade. Her body, once so vibrant with life, becomes frail. She loses her appetite, and her sleep is haunted by the shadows of memories that refuse to let her go. She is no longer just a widow—she is a woman waiting for something, though she cannot name it herself. It's as if her very spirit is being drawn toward something she cannot escape, something only Anand can provide.

Her decline is not just physical. It is spiritual, as if the very act of her being alive without him has become an affront to the life they once shared. I think of **the last days of Cleopatra**, when she chose to end her life after the fall of her kingdom and the loss of her lover, **Mark Antony**. Her heart, broken by the death of her love and the empire she could no longer control, stopped beating with the same strength. She, too, became a shadow of what she once was, a woman whose soul, like Mahima's, was caught between worlds—still anchored in the present but yearning for the past, for something that could never return.

One night, as the cold wind howls outside, Mahima falls ill. A fever grips her, and her once steady heart now races, erratic and uncertain. Her family panics, rushing to her side, but even they know that something more is at play. Mahima is no longer just ill. She is broken in ways they cannot fix.

I, too, feel the weight of it. I see it clearly now. She is not just grieving the loss of her husband. She is grieving for herself, for the pieces of her soul that were lost when Anand departed. The love that held her together is no longer there, and without it, her spirit begins to disintegrate.

I remember **the death of Queen Victoria**, when the British Empire itself seemed to waver after the passing of the monarch who had seen it through an entire era. After her husband, Prince Albert's death in 1861, she fell into an irreversible grief, and the world she knew started to collapse around her. Her mourning, deep and unresolved, left a nation in disarray, as it was forced to reckon with the loss of its matriarch. Just as Victoria lost herself in the wake of her husband's death, Mahima, too, seems to be losing herself, not only in her grief but in the very essence of life itself.

She drifts, like a leaf caught in a quiet, unstoppable current. And just as quietly, she slips away from this world—her breath shallow, her heart stilling, the last flicker of her life fading like the dimming of a candle.

In the stillness of her passing, I feel her presence shift. It is not sorrow, nor pain, but a release—a quiet letting go.

The death of Socrates in 399 BC comes to mind. The philosopher, facing execution by drinking hemlock, spoke of his acceptance of death, his body slowly shutting down as he awaited the inevitable. The light of his life dimmed as he walked calmly towards his end, embracing the quiet release that awaited him. Socrates' final moments were peaceful, a release from the pain of existence, and as Mahima passes, I feel that same peace, the quiet resolution that comes from knowing there is nothing more to fight, nothing left to do. The world she knew is gone, and in her release, she finds a strange comfort.

Mahima has found her peace, and in that peace, she will meet Anand once more, as she had always hoped. The pieces are finally in place.

And so, I wait once again, as always, for the next journey to unfold.

6. The Eternal Night

Ravi lies in a hospital bed, his body frail, tethered to machines, his breath shallow. Around him, his parents sit in a vigil of hope, though their faces betray their weariness. The clock ticks with slow, deliberate precision, marking the passage of time that feels so surreal. But inside Ravi's mind, time has ceased to exist. The night of the accident — that night — plays on repeat, looping endlessly in the quiet chaos of his thoughts. It's like a forgotten battle fought long ago, like the struggle of a king whose name is lost to history, a battle never won, a war of the soul.

And there, within the confines of his mind, I stand. Watching. Waiting.

It is the same as it always was — and yet, it isn't. This night is both the beginning and the end, the crash and the silence after, the point of no return. And as Ravi relives the night over and over, I, Death, begin to drift. My thoughts, ever tangled with time, wander back to other moments — other nights, other deaths. I remember the night of the fall of Constantinople in 1453, when the earth trembled with the weight of empires crumbling, when the last breath of the Byzantine Empire was taken under the crushing walls of the Ottomans. I was there, standing silent as Mehmed II watched the city fall, his eyes heavy with the weight of conquest and blood. It was not so different from this, from the suffocating finality that looms over Ravi's bed. A kingdom of hope crushed under the weight of fate.

Ravi's mother reaches out, smoothing his hair, as though trying to brush away the memories that haunt him. "Beta, wake up," she whispers, her voice trembling, desperate for the boy she once knew.

But he does not wake. He cannot. Not yet.

The night continues to stretch before him, and the cycle repeats. Each time, he finds himself in the car, racing down the road. He remembers the laughter, the warm breeze through the window, and then the sudden crash. But with each replay, it changes. The faces in the car become unfamiliar, like warriors in a forgotten battle. One moment, it is Mahima beside him; the next, it is a nameless soldier from the Battle of Hastings, who rode with Harold Godwinson, his armor clattering as he faced William the Conqueror's army. The death of that soldier echoed through the pages of history like a distant drumbeat. He died for a cause, for an empire, yet in his last moments, he was just a man, lost in the chaos. And perhaps that is what Ravi is—just another man, lost in the chaos of his own mind, trying to make sense of the shattered pieces of his existence.

I can feel it now, the same helplessness that hangs in the air. The same stillness. In a faraway time, I stood on the battlefield at Waterloo in 1815, watching Napoleon's final defeat. The Emperor, once so full of ambition, now shattered on the ground, his empire crumbling like a castle of sand beneath the storm's wrath. There was no escape for him either, no way to outrun the inevitable. How many have tried, only to end where they began? I remember how his eyes searched for answers, but there were none to find. I had taken him, and all that remained was the silence.

In the hospital room, Ravi's father stares out the window, his face a mask of quiet concern. "Why won't he wake up?" he murmurs to no one in particular. "He's strong. He has to fight. He can't leave us like this."

But Ravi is fighting, just not the fight his father believes he is. Ravi is not fighting with his body, but with his soul, locked in an endless loop. The crash, the crash, again and again. It's a spiral that takes him further away with every repetition, each cycle dragging him deeper into a void. This, too, I have seen before. During the reign of King Richard III, when the Battle of Bosworth took place in 1485, Richard fought a battle he knew he could not win, and yet he fought it to the bitter end. His body was never found—lost to the muck of history, as if the earth itself had swallowed him up. Perhaps he, too, was caught in an endless loop, his spirit trapped in that moment on the battlefield, fighting battles that never ended.

Ravi's mother bends down, pressing a kiss to his forehead, her tears mingling with his feverish skin. "I know you're still here," she whispers. "Come back to us, my son."

But the loop continues. The night replays itself, like a tragic tale that cannot be rewritten. His mind, still recovering from the trauma, grasps for something familiar, something real, but it is lost—further away with each passing second. It is like the stories of the Pharaohs of Egypt—men who ruled with power and pride, but when their time came, they were consumed by the sands of time. I remember the tomb of Ramses II, the Pharaoh whose heart was buried in the desert, whose name would become a whisper in the wind. Did he know, when he lay in his deathbed, that he would be forgotten? That his empire would crumble like a child's playhouse? The Pharaoh could not escape death, and Ravi cannot escape this loop of time.

I watch as his body lies still, but his mind races. His heart struggles, but his soul is lost in the abyss. Each moment stretches endlessly, a never-ending spiral of death and rebirth, like the fall of Rome in 476 AD.

The city was not conquered in a day; no, it was consumed over time, bit by bit, until nothing remained but the echoes of a once great civilization. Ravi's mind, too, is consumed — bit by bit, until all that is left is the crash. The faces. The darkness. The silence.

His father watches him, the flickering of the candlelight dancing across his face, his features soft with worry. "Come back to us, Ravi. Please," he whispers again, the words weighted with the knowledge of a father who cannot save his son from the grip of fate.

But I know. I know that fate has already sealed its deal.

In time, Ravi will awaken — but not in the way they expect. Not in the way they hope. The pieces of his fate, much like the pieces of empires before him, are scattered. They will never fall back together the way they once were.

And I, Death, will watch as the pieces shift and turn, as history repeats itself, and as Ravi's soul — forever bound to the cycle — finds its way.

For now, all I can do is wait.

7. The Spiral Deepens

Ravi lay in bed, his body slowly recovering from the injuries of that fateful night, but his soul remained fractured beyond repair. The days and nights in the hospital stretched endlessly, as sterile walls bore witness to his torment. His mother sat by his side, her lips constantly moving in prayer, but Ravi had no words to offer. He was too consumed by guilt to ask for forgiveness, even from a God he had not believed in until now.

Each night was the same: a replay of the accident in vivid, agonizing detail. The rain hammered down on the windshield, the road slick and unforgiving. Anand's laughter echoed in the car, followed by the deafening screech of tires, the shattering glass, and then — silence. That oppressive, eternal silence.

And now, Mahima was gone too. His parents told him in hushed voices, their eyes brimming with tears, but Ravi barely reacted. What could he say? What could he feel? His actions had not just ended Anand's life; they had extinguished Mahima's light as well, leaving two children orphaned in the cruelest way.

The weight of his guilt pressed on him like a stone, crushing his chest until every breath felt like a battle.

"God spared you for a reason," his mother whispered one day, placing a trembling hand on his arm. Her voice was a fragile thread of hope, trying to tether him to the world. "You must find that reason, Ravi."

Her words echoed long after she left the room. What reason could there possibly be for his survival? Was this some divine punishment, to live while Anand and Mahima were gone?

When his mother handed him a copy of the Bhagavad Gita, Ravi accepted it wordlessly. It felt heavy in his hands, as if the weight of the ages was bound within its pages. He flipped through it that night, not expecting anything but silence. Instead, his eyes fell on a verse that seemed to speak directly to him:

"The soul is neither born nor does it ever die; nor having once existed, does it ever cease to be. The soul is eternal, unborn, undying, and primeval." (Bhagavad Gita 2:20)

The words stirred something deep within him. Anand's soul, Mahima's soul—they had not truly perished. They had merely moved on, leaving behind the broken shells of their bodies. The thought was both comforting and terrifying. If their souls were eternal, then so too was his guilt.

Ravi began to seek solace in the sacred text, reading its verses late into the night. He found some respite in its teachings of karma and detachment, but each lesson seemed to cut deeper into his wounds. How could he detach from the memories of that night? How could he move forward when every step felt like a betrayal of Anand and Mahima's memory?

He turned to the Quran next, searching for answers in its verses. One passage stayed with him:

"And whoever kills a believer intentionally, their recompense is Hell, wherein they will abide eternally. And Allah has become angry with them and has cursed them." (Surah An-Nisa 4:93)

The words struck him like a blow. Though he had not killed Anand and Mahima with intent, wasn't his recklessness just as damning? He had driven that night knowing he wasn't in full control. He had ignored the warnings, the dangers, and in doing so, had taken lives.

His search for peace led him to the Bible as well. One verse, in particular, lingered in his mind:

"For all have sinned and fall short of the glory of God." (Romans 3:23)

The universality of sin was supposed to bring comfort, a reminder that no one was beyond redemption. But Ravi couldn't feel redeemed. His sin wasn't just a failure of the self—it was a failure that had destroyed an entire family.

Despite his growing despair, Ravi began attending temple services. The rhythmic chants, the flicker of oil lamps, and the scent of incense brought a fleeting sense of calm. He would sit at the back, his head bowed, listening to the priests recite verses that had been spoken for centuries.

One day, as he knelt before the deity, an old priest approached him. The man's eyes were kind, his voice gentle.

"You carry a heavy burden, my son," he said, his words more observation than question.

"I do," Ravi replied, his voice hoarse. "But I can't seem to lay it down."

The priest nodded. "Perhaps you are not meant to lay it down. Some burdens must be carried, not discarded. They shape us, teach us, and in time, they transform us."

Ravi wanted to believe him, but the burden of guilt felt less like a lesson and more like a sentence.

As his physical health improved, his inner torment only deepened. He began to isolate himself further, refusing visits from friends and family. Aayan and Ankita came to see him once, their young faces etched with confusion and sadness. Ravi couldn't even look at them. How could he face the children whose parents he had taken?

The historical weight of his guilt began to intertwine with his thoughts. He remembered reading about Emperor Ashoka, who had been consumed by guilt after the Kalinga War. The bloodshed he had caused had transformed him, leading him to renounce violence and embrace Buddhism. But unlike Ashoka, Ravi felt no transformation, no enlightenment. His guilt remained a black hole, swallowing any light that tried to enter.

One night, Ravi dreamed of Mahatma Gandhi, walking the salt flats during the Dandi March. The image was hauntingly vivid: Gandhi's frail frame bent with the weight of the world's injustices, his steps resolute despite the odds. Ravi woke up with tears streaming down his face. If Gandhi could carry such immense burdens and still move forward, why couldn't he?

But the question lingered unanswered.

He returned to the Bhagavad Gita, clinging to its teachings like a drowning man clutching a lifeline. One verse stood out:

"Let not the fruits of action be your motive, nor let your attachment be to inaction." (Bhagavad Gita 2:47)

The idea of selfless action resonated with him, but it also tormented him. What action could he take to atone for what he had done? The very thought of trying to live a meaningful life felt like an insult to Anand and Mahima's memory.

Ravi's nights grew darker, his prayers more desperate. He begged God for forgiveness, for relief, for some sign that his existence had purpose. But the silence that followed was deafening. He began to wonder if the silence was the answer.

The temple became his second home, a place where he could hide from the world and confront his demons. Yet, even there, his guilt found him. One evening, as he sat by the temple's sacred pond, he stared into the water, watching his reflection ripple and distort.

"Why me?" he whispered. "Why did you let me live?"

The pond offered no reply, only the quiet rustle of leaves in the wind.

Ravi thought of the myth of Sisyphus, condemned to roll a boulder up a hill for eternity, only for it to roll back down each time he neared the summit. His life felt like that—an endless cycle of guilt and despair, with no end in sight.

As the weeks turned into months, Ravi's prayers became more fragmented. He still sought God, but the solace he had once found in scripture now eluded him. The verses felt hollow, their promises of liberation unattainable.

One verse from the Quran echoed in his mind:

"Indeed, with hardship comes ease." (Surah Ash-Sharh 94:6)

But what ease could come from this hardship? Ravi's guilt had become his identity, and he could no longer imagine a life without it.

His parents continued to worry, urging him to focus on the future, to find a way to move forward. But Ravi knew he couldn't. The past was an anchor, pulling him deeper and deeper into an ocean of despair.

One cold night, Ravi sat alone in his room, the temple bells ringing faintly in the distance. He clutched the Bhagavad Gita in his hands, its pages worn from countless readings. He thought of Anand, of Mahima, of their children. He thought of the lives he had destroyed sand the life he could no longer bear to live.

Closing his eyes, he whispered a final prayer:

"Forgive me."

8. The Final Embrace

The house was steeped in an oppressive silence, alive and pulsing with unseen weight. Ravi sat in the dim corner of his room, a small vial of poison trembling in his hand. Its clarity mocked him, its bitter promise both a lure and a threat. He had reached the end of a labyrinth, not to find freedom, but a wall he could no longer scale. His mind reeled, returning to the beginning of it all—the accident, Anand's life slipping through his hands, Mahima's slow descent into grief and eventual death.

The weight of survival pressed on his chest. Why had life chosen him to linger when all it did was crush him further? He lifted the vial, watching the liquid catch the faint light, shimmering like an invitation. Socrates' words echoed faintly in his mind, "An unexamined life is not worth living," though he wondered if it wasn't the examined life that had brought him to this unbearable clarity of his sins.

He uncorked the vial, the faint scent of bitterness reaching his nose. The world seemed to hold its breath as he tipped the poison to his lips. A shiver ran through him as he swallowed, a cold, creeping tide seeping through his body, coiling around his heart. The act was not rushed or impulsive but deliberate, as though this moment had been waiting for him all along.

Outside his home, a man stood beneath the shade of a banyan tree, his gaze fixed on the faint flicker of light through the cracked window. He had watched Ravi pacing earlier, a restless shadow moving against the faint glow of a single candle.

The man wore a threadbare kurta, his face worn and weathered, yet there was something timeless about him, something that existed both here and elsewhere. He did not approach in haste or alarm but with a deliberate calm, as though he had seen this scene unfold countless times before. When Ravi sank to the floor, clutching his chest, the man stepped forward, his movements neither hurried nor hesitant, a quiet inevitability guiding his steps.

Darkness engulfed Ravi, wrapping him in its cold embrace. At first, there was nothing — just an endless void. Then, a voice, low and steady, broke through.

"You've called me again."

Ravi's eyes fluttered open, finding himself in a boundless expanse of silver mist. The man from the banyan tree stood before him, though his form seemed to shimmer, edges indistinct as though no longer tethered to the laws of the living world.

"Who are you?" Ravi whispered, though the answer already lingered in his mind.

"I am the keeper of endings," the figure said simply. "You've met me before, though you may not have recognized me. I was there with Anand. I was there with Mahima."

Ravi sank to his knees, his voice breaking. "Then why didn't you take me? Why did you let me live?"

The figure's gaze was unreadable, neither kind nor unkind. "You were not ready. Death is not just an ending — it is a transformation. And you had lessons still to learn."

Ravi shook his head, anguish spilling out of him. "Lessons?" he spat bitterly. "What lessons could justify this suffering? I've done nothing but carry the weight of my sins. I killed Anand. I destroyed Mahima."

The figure stepped closer, its presence heavy yet serene. "You see yourself as the sole architect of their pain. But do you not see the web that binds all life? Anand's death was not your creation — it was a thread in a tapestry woven far beyond your understanding. Mahima's grief, though born of loss, was also a journey toward her reunion with Anand.

And you, Ravi, were the witness to all of it, the bearer of their stories."

Ravi's fists clenched, his body trembling. "No! I'm not a witness. I'm the cause!"

The figure did not waver. "Then why do you think I allowed you to live this long? Why do you think the poison did not claim you immediately?"

Ravi's breath hitched, his hands clutching his chest as he felt the slow burn spreading through his veins. The poison was not swift or merciful. It lingered, forcing him to confront every moment of his final act with unrelenting clarity.

Without warning, the silver mist shifted. Ravi stood on a vast battlefield, the cries of soldiers ringing out around him. Arrows rained from the sky, and the ground beneath him was soaked with blood.

"This is Kurukshetra," the figure said, gesturing to the chaos. "A place where countless lives ended, and yet, their deaths were not in vain. They were part of a greater story, a dharma that transcended their suffering."

The cries faded, replaced by the haunting recitation of scripture. The figure's voice resonated in the air: "Yada Yada Hi Dharmasya Glanirbhavati Bharata |"

(Bhagavad Gita 4:7) "Whenever there is a decline in righteousness, I manifest myself."

Ravi found himself in another place, the air heavy with incense and ancient wisdom. A man sat cross-legged, trembling hands tracing lines onto parchment. "This is Al-Ma'mun, Caliph of Baghdad," the figure explained. "He, too, drowned in guilt for the blood spilled during his reign. Yet his legacy was not his guilt but the House of Wisdom he left behind."

The figure turned to Ravi, its tone unyielding yet compassionate. "Do you see now? Death is not about blame or redemption. It is about continuation — about what is left behind."

Ravi's tears fell freely. "I have nothing to leave behind. No wisdom, no legacy. Only pain."

The figure knelt before him. "Even pain has its purpose. Your suffering has given you understanding, and that understanding is what you carry into the next realm."

In Ravi's trembling hands appeared a jasmine flower, pristine and unbroken, its fragrance untouched by the world's cruelty. He stared at it, the weight of its symbolism pressing upon him.

"Will it hurt?" he asked, his voice barely above a whisper.

"No more than the life you've endured," the figure replied, "and far less than the guilt you've carried."

Ravi placed the flower at the figure's feet. As he did, he felt his body begin to dissolve — not in agony, but in quiet, peaceful release. The boundaries of his existence faded, and for the first time, the crushing weight of silence lifted.

The figure extended its hand, and Ravi took it without hesitation. Together, they stepped into the mist, leaving behind the echoes of his sins and the pain of the living world.

The jasmine flower remained, its delicate fragrance lingering in the still air — a quiet testament to Ravi's final surrender, his journey toward an unknown eternity.

Epilogue

The mist settles now, quiet and eternal, as I close this chapter of yet another life. Ravi's story is not unlike so many I have witnessed—fragile, chaotic, and burdened by the weight of choices and chance. Yet, it is unique in its own way, as each life inevitably is.

I am the keeper of endings, but endings are never truly final. They ripple across time, across hearts, across the unseen threads that bind existence. Ravi sought peace in the quiet embrace of death, but peace is not something I grant; it is something you carry within you, or fail to find at all.

Through his pain, his struggle, and his surrender, Ravi has found his place beyond the veil. In the end, even his darkest acts were not the totality of who he was. His grief, his guilt, and even his fleeting hope were threads woven into the same fabric.

As I sit now, writing this in the ledger of existence, I think back to all the lives I have touched—not just Ravi, or Mahima, or Anand, but countless others. The pharaoh who faced his tomb with dignity as the Nile whispered its ancient secrets. The soldier who stood firm at Agincourt, his breath fogging the damp English air, a prayer frozen on his lips. The mother in the plague years who kissed her child's brow one last time and laid her in the earth with trembling hands.

I remember them all.

I have been called many names across millennia—Thanatos, Azrael, Yamraj, the Reaper, the Ferryman. You know me as Death. But to me, you are far more than names and titles; you are the stories I carry, the echoes that linger long after your final breath has faded.

Know this: I am neither your enemy nor your savior. I am simply the inevitable, the bridge between what was and what will be. I come not to punish or to reward, but to guide. And when your time comes, as it will for all, I will sit by your side, not as a stranger, but as an old friend who has walked this path many times before.

Until then, live.

Live in the chaos, the joy, the grief, and the love that is uniquely yours. Carry the weight of your silences, but do not let them drown you. Speak when you can, forgive when you must, and find meaning in the moments, however fleeting.

And when your story ends, I will be there, pen in hand, to write your name in my book, to carry your whispers into eternity.

For in every ending, there is a beginning waiting to unfold.

— Death